DINOSAURS, BEWARE!

✚ A Safety Guide ✚

Marc Brown and Stephen Krensky

Little, Brown and Company
Boston   Toronto   London

For endangered species everywhere

Library of Congress Cataloging in Publication Data

Brown, Marc Tolon.
Dinosaurs, beware!

Summary: Approximately sixty safety tips are demonstrated by dinosaurs in situations at home, during meals, camping, in the car, and in other familiar places.
1. Children's accidents — Prevention — Juvenile literature. [1. Safety] I. Krensky, Stephen.
II. Title.

HV675.5.B76 363.1'075 82—15207
AACR2

ISBN 0-316-11228-3
ISBN 0-316-11219-4 (pbk)

HC: 10 9 8 7
PB: 10 9

JOY STREET BOOKS ARE PUBLISHED BY LITTLE, BROWN AND COMPANY (INC.)

*Published simultaneously in Canada
by Little, Brown & Company (Canada) Limited*

PRINTED IN THE UNITED STATES OF AMERICA

Contents

At Home	4
In the Yard	8
During Meals	10
In Case of Fire	12
With Animals	14
On Wheels	16
At the Playground	18
When Camping	20
In the Car	21
At the Beach	22
On Short Trips	24
Giving First Aid	26
In Cold Weather	28
At Night	30

At Home

Don't play with matches.

Keep toys off the stairs.

4

Never play with electric sockets and plugs. They can shock you.

Keep a list of important phone numbers handy in case of an emergency.

Never play with the things stored under sinks or in medicine cabinets. They can make you very sick.

If an adult isn't home, don't let strangers into the house. Tell them to come back later.

7

In the Yard

Always put tools back where they belong.

Don't climb on thin branches.

During a thunderstorm, stay out of water and away from trees.
Lightning often strikes in both places.

During Meals

Chew well before swallowing.

Don't lean back too far in your chair.

Pay attention when using a sharp knife.

Don't gulp hot foods. Taste them slowly.

11

In Case of Fire

Get outside as fast as possible, and don't stop to take along your favorite things.

If fire or heavy smoke is blocking your door, shout for help out the window.

If smoke is making you cough, crawl along the floor. The air down there will be easier to breathe.

Have a planned meeting place outside for your family. You'll know quickly if anyone is missing.

With Animals

Be very careful around a mother animal and her young. She may think you want to hurt them.

Some animals will not be friendly.

Watch out!

Never move an injured animal by yourself.

Don't feed strange animals.

On Wheels

Use reflectors and lights for riding at night.

Don't show off.

Warn others of your approach with a bell or horn.

Obey all signs and traffic lights, and cross only at corners or crosswalks.

At the Playground

Stay alert while helping your friends learn new tricks.

Look before you leap.

Don't get on or off playground equipment suddenly.

When Camping

Learn which plants are poisonous to touch, and never taste strange berries, nuts, or mushrooms.

Stay on marked trails.

Put out smoldering embers. They might start a new fire.

n the Car

Always wear seat belts. If the car stops short, you won't keep going.

Don't play games with the driver.

Keep your head and arms inside the windows.

At the Beach

Protect yourself from sunburn.

Wear a life jacket on a boat. It will keep you afloat if the boat doesn't.

Swim in pairs, and don't swim out over your head. A friend can warn you of danger.

Never overload a boat or raft.

On Short Trips

Always let someone know where you're going.

If you get lost, ask a police officer for directions.

Walk on the sidewalk, not in the street.

Don't take rides from strangers.

Carry your address, phone number, and some money in a safe place.

Giving First Aid

Clean a dirty scrape with soap and water before covering it with a bandage.

Put ice on a small burn to make it feel better and heal faster.

Pull out splinters with tweezers.

Call an adult in case of serious injury.

Cover a bee sting with mud or ice to soothe the itching and keep down the swelling.

In Cold Weather

Dress warmly, and go inside as soon as you get cold.

Never skate or walk on thin ice.

Don't make tunnels under the snow. They could fall in on you.

Make sure the coast is clear.

At Night

If you hear strange noises, call an adult to investigate.

Never assume you know where everything is. Turn on a light.

Wear light-colored clothing when you go outdoors so you can be seen easily.

Always use a flashlight.

So, dinosaurs, beware! Wouldn't you rather be safe than sorry?